P9-DII-311

SEP 1993

THE MOON
AND THE OYSTER

Written by Donia Blumenfeld Clenman

Illustrated by Laszlo Gal

Orca Book Publishers

NORTHPORT PUBLIC LIBRARY
NORTHPORT, NEW YORK

Text copyright © 1992 Donia Blumenfeld Clenman
Illustrations copyright © 1992 Laszlo Gal

Publication assistance provided by The Canada Council.
All rights reserved.

Orca Book Publishers
PO Box 5626 Stn. B
Victoria, B.C. Canada
V8R 6S4

Design by Christine Toller
Printed and bound in Hong Kong

Canadian Cataloguing in Publication Data
Clenman, Donia Blumenfeld, 1927–
The moon and the oyster

ISBN 0-920501-83-4

I. Gal, Laszlo. II. Title.
PS8555.L45M6 1992   jC813'.54   C92-091499-3
PZ7.C445Mo 1992

For Kim Hélène who smiles at the world
and
All the children who love our wondrous home
DBC

To Lynda and Janet with thanks
LG

$\mathcal{A}$ long time ago, in a world where toy hearts burned with love and mermaids died of heartbreak, a fisherman's young daughter stood barefoot on a darkened beach. Fearfully, she looked up at the sky. She thought of her father who had left on a long trip. Above her, the crescent of a

newborn moon shimmered like a pale candle.

"Please God," she whispered, "watch over my father. Give him starry nights and a bright moon, and bring him back to me safely."

And as the daughter waited, a very young oyster slept peacefully in the ocean, rocked by the warm waters of the lagoon. He was no different from any other oyster, except for the length and delicacy of his antennae and his strange habit of admiring the commonplace. No matter what he saw, a damsel fish, a piece of black coral, the shadow of an albatross or the silhouette of a man, he would pause and exclaim, "How wonderful!"

One day, a shaft of light made him tremble. It was strange the way it shone, seemingly serene on the surface, yet slicing the waters like a shark's fin.

"Did you see it? Something on the water, so bright and deep, caressing and cutting at the same time. Do you know what it is?"

But oysters are not particularly curious creatures.

"The water is warm and soft today," said one.

"Don't bother me. Can't you see I am busy opening and closing my shell?" said another.

The young oyster sighed, then moved away. "Perhaps tomorrow," he whispered. "Perhaps tomorrow I will see it again."

The moon was full and round. Lazily, she sailed across the sky, island hopping from cloud to cloud. At last she came to rest on the surface of the ocean. "There are two of me now," she said, "but then, I am so many things. A crescent at my birth, a semi-circle, a great circle and then a sliver like a dying candle. I tremble when I disappear in my eclipses. And yet,

when I rock the tides, the oceans listen to my bidding. When I am at my brightest, the sky shimmers and glows."

She looked at herself again and spread her luminous hair like a feather-star. "A drop pearl on my forehead would be very becoming," she added.

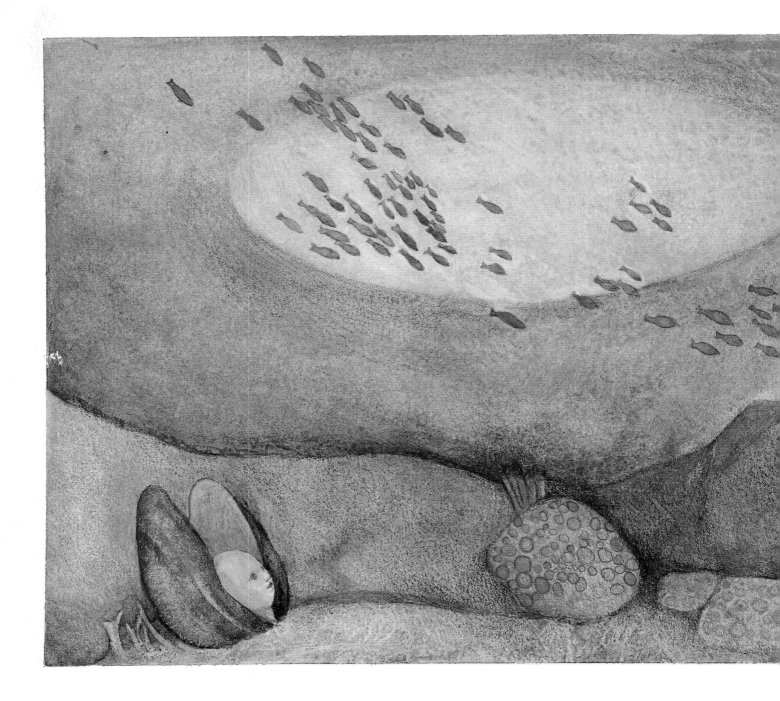

Down below, the young oyster opened his eyes and blinked, almost blinded by the strange glow. The light, a perfect circle, floated on the surface like a relaxed swimmer. The humble bottom of the lagoon with its dull sand now sparkled like a coral reef. If I could only touch it, he thought, stretching his little body.

"Perhaps, if I turn to the right . . . No, it's on the left now . . . there, in this circle . . . that circle? Oh, how dizzy I feel!"

But no matter what the oyster did, he could neither position himself under the light nor feel its glow. Swifter than a rainbow wrasse, it shifted with each wave, moving away from him in a strange game of hide-and-seek. Then, a shimmering pool of silver and ivory, it lingered for a while and disappeared. The young oyster knew he was in the presence of magic and longed to understand.

For the rest of the month he watched. How it changed shape!
Sometimes it became a crescent like the arched body of a blue fusilier,
bigger like a pearly butterfly fish, then rounder like a royal empress angel.
The night it again became a perfect globe, he couldn't contain himself any
longer and opened his mouth in wonder.

The old oyster watched him, at once amused and annoyed. "Haven't
you seen the moon before?" she asked. "And close your mouth. You might

swallow something you would regret."

"How beautiful the moon is," sighed the young oyster, turning toward the light.

"Well she's rather common. A crescent, a doughnut, a doughnut, a crescent. Always the same."

"Oh no, she's never the same. And she changes everything around us. Even your shell now has a lovely sheen."

"Well, so it does..." the old oyster was rather flattered, "but we oysters can make little moons ourselves, every bit as beautiful."

"What do you mean?" asked the young oyster.

"If you swallow a speck of sand or a tiny pebble no larger than a grain of sand, it will grow inside you and become a silver pearl just as fine as any moon. Bluish pebbles with pinkish tips make the most beautiful of all pearls, drop pearls, very rare and hard to find. And our pearls last forever, handed down from generation to generation. They don't just come and go like the moon."

"I would love to have a little moon inside me," said the young oyster. "What do I need to do to get one?"

"There is a sad part to it," answered the old oyster, "for the sand will grow and harden inside you, delicate on the outside but like a stone fish inside. It will make you sick. Men will hunt you. You may die from it. So keep your mouth closed and stop daydreaming," she added gruffly.

"How wondrous!" exclaimed the little oyster. "For anything so beautiful I would gladly give my life."

"Moon, oh Moon! Come to me! I'm only a humble mollusk, but come to me!" he cried out fervently, night after night, but in vain. Occasionally she would send him a tiny pool of light, then vanish.

"Moon, oh Moon! Great Empress! I'll make you a silver pearl, the most perfect drop pearl, but come to me!"

The night was very dark when she suddenly appeared, immense and luminous. He trembled in her presence.

"Am I not beautiful?" said the moon. "And I don't even wear any jewels."

"You could not be more beautiful than you are."

"Still a pearl would go well with my complexion," she continued. "A drop pearl would hold my hair in place and it would shine brightly in the night sky."

"May I touch you?" asked the little oyster timidly.

"But I am an enigma," she said. "No one can touch a mystery."

Day after day the little oyster sifted the sandy bottom of the lagoon. "So many pebbles!" he cried out. Most lay still, heaped up in small dunes, others, shifting and restless, formed long furrows like schools of silversides. At times, whipped by winds and waves, they whirled madly.

Once, he thought he'd found it. "Here, that's just the right pebble!" he exclaimed excitedly, "A perfect pink and blue tip!"

It was only a short distance away. He struggled as fast as he could to

reach it but in vain. "It's gone!" he cried. Perhaps he had been mistaken. Perhaps the waves shipped it away.

But he did not give up. Day after day he continued his search. Because he moved slowly, he was able to cover only a small area at a time. "How I wish I were a swift bird fish!" he cried. "If only I were a nimble flute fish and not a clumsy mollusk! If only . . . if only . . . "

Soon after a violent storm arose. All the creatures in the sea took shelter, but the little oyster still searched for the perfect blue pebble. But no matter where he turned, the bluish speck was not to be found.

The little oyster grew tired. He began to fear he might never find what he needed. Discouraged at last by the immensity of white and gray bottom, he was overcome by a great weariness. "Nothing but sand and pebbles. Sand and pebbles," he wept.

"You shouldn't be out in this weather," scolded the old oyster.

"I'm not afraid of the storm!" he shouted, weeping yet still defiant.

"It isn't just the storm. We have enemies, little one. Starfish and skates lurk among seaweeds and eelgrass. Snaketails bury themselves in the crevices of rock and coral or lie in wait at the bottom of the sea. They love to eat little daydreaming oysters. So be careful. We oysters must be practical creatures. Come with me!"

"I can't," he replied.

She looked at him with pity, and then puzzled that he would not follow her, she scuttled off looking for shelter.

Some days later, a new, barely visible crescent appeared on the horizon. It trembled a little, a luminous curve of beauty. The young oyster laboured on, searching the bottom intently, when a tiny current stirred the sand. Unexpectedly, something blue and pink appeared before him. At once, he sprang into action, opened his mouth wide and swallowed it. Its sharp point stung him like the lance of a sea anemone. "How it burns!" he cried out and sat down waiting for the pain to subside. It passed after a while, and a wave of happiness enveloped him.

For some time he felt no different. Then a kind of heaviness settled in his body. He had always been deliberate in his movements, but now he

moved even more slowly and found it difficult to catch up with the oysters. Once, he fell asleep in the middle of his dinner.

"Aren't you well?" asked the old one.

"Just tired," he replied.

"Still daydreaming, little one?" She eyed him anxiously.

"My Moon is beautiful," he murmured.

"So is a brittle star and a feather-star," she said sternly, "but their bodies can squeeze themselves through the narrowest crevice. And they are hungry for oysters, pearls, everything. Be careful little one."

"But I love her," he answered.

The vague pressure became a pain, occasional at first, then sharper and more persistent. The pearl in the young oyster's body grew and matured. He slept fitfully, waking only when he felt a glow on the waters. He lost all sense of time. In his dreams, with only a single lantern fish to light his way, he wandered in a terrifying darkness, crying, "Moon! Moon!"

The small, soft body hardened. The pain grew and spread. He knew his end was near. The pearl was ripe. He was beside himself with worry. Unless she came to him, all would be in vain. "Great empress! Come to me!"

At last, in all her majesty she appeared, her face carved ivory, hair silver translucence. For the first time she did not elude him, and her touch was sweet, soft and gentle, for she was moved by his devotion. "Here I am, my little oyster. Can you hear me?"

"How beautiful you are," he whispered. "I've missed you so much. What do you do in the sky, my Moon?"

"I shine on sleeping children's faces, light the way for stranded fishermen and inspire people to love."

"Your pearl is ready."

"Are you in much pain, little one?" She bent over him and her face shone with kindness. "I know something about dying too," she added sadly.

"Touch me, my Moon."

She kissed the young oyster, and he felt light and giddy as if carried by the gentlest breeze.

At that moment his shell split open, releasing an immense pearl, bluer than the restless sea, warmer than the rising sun.

"How exquisite it is!" the moon exclaimed. "I'll always wear it and think of you, my little oyster." She placed it on her forehead, and he felt himself lifted as she rose, the drop pearl trembling in her hair.

"Farewell, little oyster," she whispered as his shell cracked and he slowly sank to the bottom of the ocean.

And in the world above, the fisherman's young daughter still waited for her father. Night after night she kept her watch. But the sea was restless and the moon a pale crescent waxing and waning.

Gradually, the waters grew calm. And one night, as she scanned the dark horizon, an immense moon lit the sky and the girl saw a familiar boat gliding softly on a silvery road.

"Father, Father," she cried, running to him, "it has been so dark and I've missed you so much. But you are home . . . you are home!" And she clapped her hands with joy.

The moon spread her luminous hair and the drop pearl trembled on her forehead as she watched the fishermen unload their cargo, great nets of glistening mussels and oysters.

NORTHPORT PUB LIBRARY

0605 9100 024 577 8

SEP   1993

Northport - E. Northport Public Library
151 Laurel Avenue
Northport, N. Y. 11768
261-6930